Spirit of Life

Sumana Roy Chowdhury

Ukiyoto Publishing

Contents

Voices On The Roof

(Loosely based on true events)

The taxi came to a halt in front of a nondescript four-storied building, situated about three hundred meters up a leafy lane which was set off from the crowded main road. Even though it was in the middle of a busy working day; this lane had a decidedly desolate feel to it. Aparna peered out of the window of the car to look at what-was-to-be her new home and turned around to look at Mrs. Mukherjee with a smile. Her mother nodded indulgently at the 23-year old girl while casting an appraising glance at the building in front of them, evidently not sharing her daughter's enthusiasm about the new abode. The ladies had arrived from Kolkata to Bangalore earlier that day and had managed to fight the infamous city traffic to reach their destination that was located in a suburb of the city. They were in Bangalore for the first-time and like most 8people who were new to the city, through their journey from the airport to the house, they and had looked on in wonder at the snarling, chaotic traffic; the harrowed commuters who bravely swerved their bikes through the maze of cars and buses and the demotivated traffic policemen who stood listlessly swaying their arms in no specific direction, evidently having given up on all hopes of controlling the traffic a long time ago.

The decision for Aparna and her mother to come to Bangalore had been a recent one. The girl had completed her master's degree in Chemistry from a reputed college in Kolkata and given her good grades, she had almost immediately landed a job at a MNC in Bangalore. This was cause for celebration but also for considerable discussion and debate. The weeks' following the job offer had passed in a flurry of activities at the Mukherjee household as the couple prepared for their only daughter's departure to a new city. After looking through several rental websites and a lot of heated discussions, in which Aparna had little to no say; her parents had finally zeroed in on a house that they deemed as somewhat suitable for their daughter to live in. This house was a one BHK apartment that was nicely located within walking distance of the office and came with a surprisingly low rent by Bangalore standards which fit in well with Aparna's fresher's salary. Since this was the first time that Aparna was leaving the comforts of her home, Mrs. Mukherjee had declared that she would accompany her daughter to Bangalore to live with her for the first few months. This practice was not unheard of in traditional Bengali families and despite her hapless daughter's many protests, Mrs. Mukherjee had stayed firm in her decision.

"But Ma, I won't be alone if you think about it. Piyali will be joining me in ten days' time", wailed Aparna trying to dissuade her mother from putting a stop, to what she had fancied to be her first flight to freedom, out of the clutches of her over-protective mother.

Piyali was Aparna's best friend and daughter of the Mukherjee's neighbor in Kasba, a posh South-Kolkata locality, where the girls had grown up. Aparna and Piyali had been inseparable since childhood; having attended the same school and college; and now they had landed their first job in the same firm in Bangalore as well. Naturally they had decided that they would share their accommodation in the new city and the girls had grand plans of having uninterrupted night-time chats, frequenting the famous Bangalore pubs and binge watching their favorite web-series together. But it certainly looked like destiny had other plans in store...

"That girl is as irresponsible as you are Apu", said Mrs. Mukherjee in a matter-of-fact tone. "The two of you require some adult supervision and I have discussed this with Piyali's mother as well. So, the topic is closed. I am going to accompany you to Bangalore and that's that!"

So that had been that and now, a month later, Aparna and the plump Mrs. Mukherjee alighted from the air-conditioned confines of the taxi to be greeted by the pleasant Bangalore climate. Piyali was to join them ten days later. The women stood outside the apartment building and made the customary comments about how despite the horrific traffic, the climate in Bangalore was wonderful versus the oppressive Kolkata heat in the month of August.

Aparna stretched her hands and looked around to see the caretaker of the building, who was a middle-aged, dark complexioned man; wearing a blue uniform and three horizontal white stripes on his forehead, as was customary to South Indian men. He was sitting on a rickety plastic chair near the front door, lazily swatting at flies with a folded newspaper. On seeing Aparna and her mother get off the taxi, he promptly came forward to help them unload their four heavy suitcases from the vehicle and introduced himself as Mahadev, the watchman-cum-caretaker of the building.

Presently, Mahadev panted heavily as he lugged three suitcases all the way up to the fourth floor, which was where the apartment that Aparna had rented was situated. Aparna noticed that the building smelled of fresh paint and was obviously new, as the advertisement on the website had mentioned. However, it seemed to have no other residents and the sharp Mrs. Mukherjee was quick to pick up on this.

"Does no one else live here, Mahadev?", she asked between pants as she climbed the stairs, following her daughter and the caretaker. Although Mrs. Mukherjee did not carry any suitcases with her but the task of carrying her weight up the stairs was not to be considered a trivial one.

"It's a new apartment madam. It will take some time for people to come to live here", replied Mahadev. He then added, "but the apartment next door also belongs to the same builder and it is now full, so you will have neighbors…"

Mrs. Mukherjee nodded as she continued the tedious climb up the stairs while she muttered under her breath about the lack of an elevator.

"Ma…come quickly and see. What a beautiful view we have from here", called out Aparna, who was nimbler and had managed to reach the fourth floor already along with the one suitcase that she had volunteered to carry.

Her mother joined her in sometime, wiping her forehead with the end of her cotton saree despite the moderate city temperature. She gasped at the sight of her daughter leaning from the balcony taking in the surroundings. There was an empty field behind the building which was filled with tall eucalyptus trees that swayed gently in the pleasant breeze. Unfortunately, Mrs. Mukherjee's maternal instincts made her unaware of the beauty of her surroundings and she rapidly walked over to Aparna to firmly pull her back.

"What are you doing Apu? Don't lean on the railing like that. What if it breaks? You won't survive a fall from here. Do you want to break your neck?"

Her daughter rolled her eyes, "Come on Ma. I am not a kid anymore. I will be starting my first job tomorrow. Treat me like an adult", she jerked her long hair back from her small, oval face and excitedly rubbed her palms together. The older woman looked at her daughter's pretty face and wide brown eyes. She thought for the millionth time how similar she used to be as a girl. However, before she could ponder further about her lost youth her protective instincts came back with a vengeance. She hardened her expression and opened her mouth to reprimand Aparna further, when the girl was saved from the sermon by the timely intervention from Mahadev who called out to them…

"Madam, Didi…I have unlocked the door. Please come and see the apartment…"

The apartment had a spacious living room which was furnished with a two-seater sofa along the wall at the far end of the room, a center-table and a wall-mounted television opposite to the sofa set. The French windows in the living room opened on to a small balcony that overlooked the field with the eucalyptus trees. There was an adequate kitchen which was furnished with wooden cabinets, a refrigerator and a gas stove. A short corridor led out of the living room in to the bedroom which had a double bed, a wooden cupboard, a dressing table with a thin mirror and an attached bathroom. Although Aparna looked happy with the new house, her mother, who was used to living in her spacious two-storied house in Kasba, pursed her lips in dissatisfaction.

"Can we get hot water here?", she asked as she looked suspiciously at the tiny geyser that was mounted on the wall in the bathroom.

"Yes madam. And there is running water for 24 hours, back-up power in case of power failures, a gas cylinder in the kitchen and a dish antenna for the television", rattled off Mahadev, seeming keen to sell the house to the new tenants. He paused and on seeing the dubious look on Mrs. Mukherjee's face, he quickly continued, "you will also find a kirana shop if you walk down the lane and I have had a maid clean the house this morning. She will come back tomorrow morning and you can speak with her about her wages etc."

The mention of a maid caused Mrs. Mukherjee's expression to soften a little and she followed Mahadev out in to the living room.

"Ok…ok", she said as she turned on the living room fan and plopped down on the sofa.

"Madam, I will be downstairs. Please call me if you need anything", said Mahadev, walking towards the door. As he reached the door, he turned and added in a lower tone, "I leave at eight in the evening, but I will lock the grill downstairs and leave the keys with you so that in case you want to go out you can open the lock through the grill…although it might be better to stay indoors in the evenings…"

"What's that Mahadev-da?", asked Aparna her ears suddenly pricking up, "if you leave then there should be a night watchman, no?"

The man averted his eyes and mumbled, "No Didi…there will be no one here at night, b-but this is a safe neighborhood…"

The mother and daughter exchanged looks but before either of them could recover and speak, the caretaker had shut the front door and disappeared down the stairs.

A terrific snore from Mrs. Mukherjee caused her daughter to be jolted awake for the umpteenth time that night. She sighed irritably and reached out for the phone under her pillow to see that it was almost one o'clock at night. The girl quietly got out of bed, collected her pillow and the bed covers and tiptoed in to the living room; intending to sleep on the sofa where she hoped that her mother's tremendous snores would not reach her. The house was in complete silence and from the position where she lay on the sofa, Aparna could see the eucalyptus trees sway in the wind through the French windows. While this had made for a pleasant view during the day; the same scenery had an eerie feel at night and she felt herself shudder. Squeezing her eyes shut, she tried to go back to sleep. She had barely dozed off; when she was awakened by a sound of pounding footsteps above her. She sat up straight and looked around, dazed. *Surely, she must have been mistaken. Who could be walking around on the roof in the middle of the night? There was no one in the building apart from her and her mother.* She chided herself for being so jittery and put it down to being in a new surrounding but just as she was about to lie back down; she heard the sounds again. There was no mistaking it this time – it was a distinct sound of footsteps on the roof directly above her. Her mind worked furiously as she sat paralyzed with fear on the sofa – *Who could it be? The apartment was empty and Mahadev had locked the grill downstairs. How then had someone managed to reach the roof above? What would she do if there were burglars? What if whoever it was upstairs decided to come down and enter their house? She and her mother would be helpless. There was no one else in the building and they knew no one in the city…*

As these thoughts swirled in her mind, Aparna strained her ears to see if she could hear any further sounds fervently hoping that the earlier sound of footsteps had been a figment of her imagination. The sound of footsteps had ceased, and no sooner had she let out a sigh of relief than she heard voices; two of them – a man's and woman's. Beads of perspiration began to line Aparna's forehead despite the cool weather. She tucked her feet beneath her and hugged them close to her body when she felt a hand tap her on the shoulder…

"Aaarrrggghhh…"

"Ssshhhh – Apu – ssshhh. It's me…don't shout. They will hear you…"

Aparna opened her eyes to see her mother next to her clutching at the end of her saree and looking as terrified as she felt. She gulped a few times to get her voice back and whispered fiercely…

"What the hell do you mean by scaring me like that Ma?"

Her mother sat down on the sofa next to her and whispered back, "Sorry, sorry. But do you hear the sounds too Apu?"

Aparna nodded, and the two women stared at each other as the whispering sounds above them seemed to grow louder. Soon they could make out snatches of the conversation...

"How could you do this to me? I trusted you so much?"

"What have I done? – You are impossible, you just don't understand..."

More footsteps...

"Are you crazy? Come back here..."

"No – I will never go back to you again..."

There were sounds of a tussle; the woman crying; an ear-splitting shriek followed by a thud and then complete silence. Aparna and her mother stared at each other wide-eyed. *Had they just witnessed someone falling off the roof?* A fall from the fourth floor on to the ground below would almost certainly lead to death. Aparna felt her heart beat so loudly that she feared that whoever was on the roof above might hear it too.

"Ma – s-something has happened upstairs. Should I go and look? Perhaps they need help?", she asked faintly. Aparna was a kind-hearted girl, always ready to help those in need but she now she was torn between fear and her will to help.

Her mother ended her dilemma by grabbing her firmly by the arm making any movement close to impossible, "Apu, you are not to go anywhere now. We will see what is to be done in the morning…"

There seemed to be nothing further to do now but wait for morning. The sounds above them had ceased and Mrs. Mukherjee presently dozed off on the sofa, once again emanating fantastic snores, while her daughter fought to stay awake for a while but eventually gave in and fell in to a fitful sleep as well.

"Well?", demanded Mrs. Mukherjee, her hands firmly planted on her hips, "If the grill was locked then how did people reach the roof upstairs? Is there any other way to reach the roof other than from the front door?"

The hapless Mahadev, stood outside their apartment door and uncomfortably shifted his weight from one foot to another. He mumbled, "No madam; there is no other way to reach the roof. As I said, you must have heard the wind…"

"The wind? It cannot be Mahadev-da", said Aparna, peering through the tiny gap that her mother's girth left in the doorway, "Both of us heard the voices clearly. I am certain that there were people upstairs and something happened last night…"

"Then perhaps it was from the apartment next door. Plenty of people live there", suggested the caretaker. "The buildings are close to each other", he trailed off.

"But even then, I should have found something when I went to look…"

An audible gasp from Mahadev caused Aparna to stop in mid-sentence.

"You went up to look at night? "

"No – I went up in the morning. I also looked all around the building and in the field behind but there was nothing…"

Mahadev sighed in relief and Mrs. Mukherjee pinned him with a suspicious look…

"Is there something that you are not telling us Mahadev?"

"N-no", he stammered, averting his eyes, "It's just that- that it's better to not go out of the house at night…"

He paused as though contemplating his next words and then seeming to make up his mind; he looked straight at Aparna and said firmly. "Didi, remember my words. Whatever happens; never open the door. This is a nice apartment and locality only if you can ignore anything that you hear at night. Do not go looking for things; I can assure you that you will not find anything. As I said, you will be fine as long as you are inside the house…"

With this Mahadev departed abruptly. A sudden gust of wind through the open door blew Aparna's hair back from her forehead and she hugged herself as she felt a chill run down her spine.

"Pihu, Apu; don't stay up very late", said Mrs. Mukherjee as she looked affectionately at the two girls who were comfortably settled on the bed that had been made for Piyali on the floor of the living room. It was past ten and Mrs. Mukherjee was preparing to retire for the night.

"I will sleep here with Pihu tonight Ma", said Aparna. "It's Sunday tomorrow so we can stay awake for longer."

Piyali had arrived in Bangalore earlier that day and the two girls had greeted each other with such enthusiasm that one would have thought that they had been separated from each other for years instead of only ten days.

"Apu, don't be awake for too long. You know that they will be here soon", said Mrs. Mukherjee to her daughter in a warning tone as she disappeared in to the bedroom inside.

Piyali stared after her.

"What does Mashima mean by 'they' will be here?", she asked her friend incredulously. "As far as I know, there is no one here apart from us."

Piyali was a spunky girl, with very different personality from her friend. She always seemed to be sure of herself and feared very little and Aparna had always admired her friend's confidence and her ability to speak her mind while she herself had been prone to self-doubt.

"It's nothing Pihu", replied Aparna quickly, trying to change the topic and to get her headstrong friend off the subject.

Luckily for her, as they had so many other things to talk about, Mrs. Mukherjee's words were soon forgotten, and the two girls chatted on oblivious of time. But as one o'clock drew closer, Aparna began to grow more and more restless as she repeatedly looked at the time on her phone.

"What is it Apu?", asked Piyali. "Why are you looking at the time?"

"It's almost one", whispered back her friend, her face pale.

"One? So, what happens at one?"

Just as Aparna was about to open her mouth to answer; both girls heard the footsteps on the roof above.

"What's that?", asked Piyali loudly.

"Ssshhh", said Aparna, clamping a hand over her friend's mouth. "This is what Ma was talking about Pihu. For the past ten nights; it has been the same routine. Just listen quietly…"

As they sat quietly; they first heard the sound of footsteps; then a whispered conversation between a man and a woman that grew louder with time; more footsteps; a woman crying; a scream followed by a thud and finally silence.

Piyali looked wide-eyed at her friend.

"What just happened Apu?", she whispered. "I think I should go outside and see…"

Apu grabbed her friends' hand and shook her head. "Don't Pihu. You won't find anything. This is over for tonight, but it will be the same routine tomorrow and the day after and the day…"

Just then a sharp knock sounded on their front door making Aparna almost choke on her words. The girls clutched each other's' hands and looked towards the door. The sound of the knock had also drawn Mrs. Mukherjee out in to the living room. The three women stood frozen, staring at each other when the knock came again. This time, it was louder.

"Please open the door", called a man's voice from outside. It sounded desperate and out-of-breath. "Please, please open the door. I need your help…"

There were a series of knocks of increasing intensity after this…

"This has never happened before Pihu", whispered Mrs. Mukherjee. "No one has knocked on the door before."

Piyali's face wore a determined expression as she looked at the two other women in the room.

"We must open the door", she said as she started towards the door. "The man outside needs our help."

"Pihu no. Please Pihu don't", begged Aparna and her mother, both of whom had jumped up after Piyali.

"Whatever it is that is out there; it does not need our help", said Aparna, looking her friend in the eye. "So please Pihu – don't…"

Piyali looked at her friend for a moment, seemingly in a dilemma.

Seeing her friend hesitate; Aparna pushed further, "Mahadev-da had told me to never open the door; no matter what. So, don't do it Pihu."

Piyali looked from her friend to Mrs. Mukherjee and the older woman vehemently shook her head.

"Please sit down Pihu. We are all alone in this building now. No one will come here till morning…"

Just as Piyali was contemplating this, the knocking on the door resumed. "Please help me", came the voice from outside, followed by sounds of sobbing.

Piyali made up her mind and resolutely shook her head. "Apu, there's a man out there and he needs our help. I can see that you are too scared to help him, but I will…"

With that she flung aside Aparna's restraining arm and strode over to the door to fling it open as Aparna and Mrs. Mukherjee stood back in the room holding on to each other. A gust of ice-cold wind entered the room as soon as the door was opened, chilling all three of them to the bone although it was in the middle of summer. There was a pitch-black darkness outside the house. The solitary light bulb that usually illuminated the corridor was in darkness. Piyali peered outside, straining her eyes to see but could detect no one.

"Hello?", she said. "Is anyone there?"

"Pihu, please come back inside", Aparna was crying now, trying hard to free her arm from her mother's grasp so that she could go and rescue her friend. "There's no one out there; believe me. Please come back inside…"

"Shut up Apu. Let me see", said Piyali and stepped outside the house. No sooner than she had stepped out of the house; a tremendous blast of wind caused the door to bang shut behind her.

"Pihu", screamed Aparna, freeing herself from her mother's clutches and running towards the door. She tried to open it, but the door was locked.

"Pihu", she cried again; desperately trying to open the door. Her mother joined her too but no matter how hard they tried, the door remained locked. Aparna was close to hysteria when her mother clutched her arm and whispered. "Apu, listen…the sounds…"

Surely enough, the sounds upstairs had started once more, although the routine seemed to have altered this time. *Footsteps; voices – a man's and a woman's; sounds of a scuffle and then a scream, followed by a sickening thud.*

Aparna screamed too and collapsed on the floor as blackness spread before her eyes.

Sense Of Purpose

Hans and his siblings were born on Big Daisy's Dairy Farm next to Bruno, the Farm's single-minded breeder bull. The birth was quick and efficient, atop a steaming pile of Bruno's crap. Unlike humans, who try avoiding shit at all costs, Hans felt privileged, and enjoyed knowing he had a wing-up on millions of other flies.

From the moment he opened his five eyes, Hans was aware of his assignment. At birth, every fly is assigned a human, animal, or object. A fly's sole job is to gather as much information as possible from their assignment. This data is then downloaded into a universal record called the Great Source. Hans had no idea who controlled this record, or where it existed, or even its purpose, just that the drive to complete his duty was a persistent itch under his thorax, certain and motivating.

A few short seconds after he emerged from Bruno's dung, Hans was flapping his wings as hard as he could westward across the pasture towards the main house. His assignment was a human, little Tommy Bates, the owner's five-year old grandson. Humans were the most difficult and dangerous of all assignments given their general stupidity and endless innate desire to destroy. Billions of flies died every year, squashed, swatted, poisoned, or plucked free of their wings. Hans knew this. But Hans gleamed with confidence, infused with the awareness that he was a brave fly, a devoted one. The universe will be a better place for all creatures the more knowledge I collect. Hans fluttered around the outside of the barn, narrowly missing a thwack from Bruno's tail that had already pummeled thousands of others. He peered down on the corpses of his brethren but kept steady. Hans thought deeply about many things during his initial travels. Mainly he wondered, as all flies wondered, when he would die. He did not fear his death, but he wanted to get things right. Hans knew his life was short yet of great importance. The more information he collected from Tommy, the more he may learn about the Great Source, the more he may contribute. And so, his brain calculated each wing flap very carefully in order to maximize the approximately 28 days of his life. Stopping only to refuel on the sweaty necks of the farm workers, the journey to Tommy took 3 full days. On the morning of the third day, the sun rose hot and glaring over the main house, and Hans spotted Tommy playing with his tiny army soldiers. The boy spotted Hans. "Hey fly! Look here!" Tommy extended a giant hand. A gentle energy emanated from the huge mass of flesh. With a small hesitation unnoticed by the boy, Hans landed on his wrist. Tommy squealed and shook his hand in a fit of excitement. Hans tumbled backwards through the morning air. The boy extended his hand again. Perhaps this silly cycle of landing and shaking and landing is important, Hans thought. All morning, Hans buzzed over the boy, making contact only to be sent whirling, much to the boy's delight. Tommy finally fell asleep beneath an apple tree, and Hans landed on his shoulder, refocusing on the assignment. Hans possessed a preordained wealth of knowledge that he used to make his observations. Instinctively, he began downloading his experiences. Tommy seems overjoyed by my presence. Tommy smells like my childhood in Bruno's feces, and watermelons. Tommy likes apples, but mostly likes to pull the apple from the tree, take a bite, and then discard it. Hans wondered if it would be a good idea to draw logical conclusions from his information. Young humans consume everything. Young humans are very loud. Young humans don't feel threatening. Hans enjoyed nighttime the most. While Tommy slept, Hans darted around the bedroom, downloading all the information he could absorb. Tommy cries out in his sleep. Tommy is comforted by a pink stuffed rabbit. Tommy doesn't like thunderstorms.

By Day 12, Hans noticed a sharp pain behind his left antenna, deep inside his brain. He had ignored the pain since Day 7, when it was only a dull throb. Perched on the windowsill, Hans peered out over the farm. A slow wave of uncertainty spread into the tips of his wings. He looked down at Tommy, who mumbled adorably in his sleep. As Hans examined the boy, he suddenly realized that the pain was related to the one word Tommy liked most. Why! Tommy asked his mother. Why! Tommy yelled at the dog. Why! Tommy whispered to his little army man.

Why, Why, Why!

The life of a fly is not to question why, Hans scolded himself, though for the first time in his life, Hans wasn't confident. By Day 14, anxiety, doubt, and existential dread consumed every inch of Hans. He had no interest in sucking the sweet sugar from a red gumdrop that Tommy dropped under his bed. Though he was born to believe in the importance of his assignment, Hans decided to leave Tommy in search for answers. I'm not a particularly young fly, but better late than never! Hans encouraged himself and flew out Tommy's open bedroom window into the humid summer evening. Just as the sun breached the horizon, Hans came upon a fly darting frantically around oneof the barn cats. The cat lounged lazily under a rusted wheelbarrow, having just consumed a field mouse.

"Brother! Hello!" Hans yelled. "I have no time for chit-chat Brother!" the busy fly replied. "I'm too busy gathering information "Yes, but why?" Hans asked.

The fly slowed for a spilt second, twisting his antennae into a horrified scowl. He buzzed close to Hans.

"What do you mean why? It's not my job to question why! I was assigned this cat. I must deliver all the information I can for the Great Source. Such is the way of the fly."

"Yes, but who is the Great Source? Why do you serve It?" Hans probed, hoping for some insight."Don't question me!" the busy fly snapped. "Why do you ask such questions? This is the way it has always been. Have you no faith? No sense of duty?" And with that, the fly turned his attention back to the cat, leaving Hans to his questions.

Discouraged yet hopeful, Hans ventured on. The next day he came upon a magnificent dogwood tree where one of his sisters sat on a fragrant blossom. "Sister, hello!" Hans called.

"Brother, welcome. Come quick…and not so loud." The fly trembled under the petals of the blossom.

"Are you okay?" Hans asked his sister in a polite whisper. "I'm trying my best to gather information from this plant, but I'm so scared that I'm not doing a good enough job. The Great Source will surely punish me." The fly wept.

"Sister, why do you think that?" Hans hovered near her under a wonderfully fragrant flower.

"I don't know, but the fear is overwhelming. I can barely enjoy anything." Hans placed a wing over his sister, trying his best to comfort her, but her fear was palpable.

Surely, the Great Source would not punish his sister for trying her best. And certainly, a life spent lived in fear would be a life wasted. Hans was perplexed. He sat for hours focusing on the spot under his left antenna that throbbed; the spot that produced both his curiosity and doubt.

Hans's sister mumbled on about her fear, all-consumed. No matter what he said or did, she could not be comforted. Hans spent the day listening, trying his best to find answers in her ramblings. When his sister finally cried herself to sleep, Hans tucked her wings under the white blossom and quietly departed.

"I am on my own journey for answers Sister, and so I must leave you."

Hans left the beautiful tree. His heavy wings moved slower in the thick twilight.

After another night of contemplating the meaning of existence, Hans came upon a fence post. An older fly sat so still upon the post that Hans thought his brother may be dead. Hans landed next to the old fly, resting his wings and six legs.

"Brother?" Hans whispered.

The old fly barely turned his head. "Hey, Brother." Hans thought his brother was the saddest, oldest fly he had ever seen.

"What are you doing here? Were you assigned this fence post?" Hans probed.

"Yeah," the old fly replied in a slow, unhurried drawl.

"I got here about a month ago, downloaded some stuff. But after two weeks, there was nothing left to download. So, I've just been sitting here, waiting. Life's a slow, passionless wait."

"What are you waiting for?" Hans questioned, though he knew. "Death, I suppose. My meeting with the Great Source. But who really cares." The old fly blinked his five eyes, each one staring blankly out over the field. Desperately, Hans questioned his brother. "Who or what is the Great Source? Why do you believe in It? Please, tell me Brother!" The old fly didn't answer. He had died.

For the first time in his life, Hans cried. Tears welled up in every eye. He wasn't upset at his brother's death, but at the lack of answers. The throb in his left antenna sent painful stabs throughout his entire body. He clenched his thorax with two of his legs so as not to throw up. I give up! I will never know the Great Source, or why a fly is a fly! I should just sit here and wait for my own death. Hans lingered for an entire day on the post, thinking of nothing. The next morning, a voice cut into his depression. Tommy and his grandparents leaned against the fence near Hans. The grandpa hoisted Tommy up on the rail so he could look out over the pasture.

"Grandpa, why is that horsie so brown? And why is the field so green? And why, why, why!" Tommy wriggled around, pointing and laughing. The old man smiled broadly and answered, "Well, my son, what do you think?" Tommy bit his lip and thought hard. "I think the horsie likes being brown, and the field decided to be green! And same with the sky!" The old couple chuckled and tousled Tommy's blond hair. Tommy's grandma leaned and kissed him on the head.

"It's always important to ask yourself why, my boy."

Hans's entire body shook with an unexplained joy upon overhearing the grandma's words. For over half his life, Hans had sought answers in others, ignoring his own intuition. What do I think? What am I telling myself? The answers are within. A great and wonderful realization swept over Hans like a cool breeze. The Great Source is me! And if the Great Source is me, then it's also within my brothers and sisters. In all things. The dogwood tree, the fence post. Even the humans. The throbbing in his antenna faded, replaced by an empty calmness. Hans started flying, without purpose, happily, and landed in the grass next to the barn where he was born. Bruno grunted from inside. Millions of his brothers and sisters whizzed around, scurrying towards their assignments. Hans sat peacefully on a small piece of glass and gazed at his reflection. A loud buzzing interrupted his meditation, and a young fly landed next to him, frantic and tired. "Brother! I have flown a long way, and I'm asking every fly I come across. Do you know where I can find the Great Source?" Hans turned to the young fly and placed a wing around her.

"Yes, Sister. Look carefully here." Hans motioned to the small bit of glass. The young fly peered at herself in the glass for a long time. Then she smiled, knowing.

Sands Of Time

It was past midnight and Janardhan Chowdhury was immersed in a book. The palatial house in which he sat was bathed in silence with all it's other members long asleep. Janardhan's wife; Niharika, their nineteen-year-old son Abhishek and all the servants of the household were fast asleep. Janardhan was sitting in the living room next to the large window that overlooked the vast backyard of their countryside home. A glistening lake was visible in the distance at the far end of yard. He was the Zamindar of the estate, a coveted position in pre-independent India. It was a position that brought with itself its share of luxuries which included the huge house in which he lived.

Janardhan enjoyed this time of the night when he was all by himself with no one to bother him. The only sound to accompany him was the distant chirping of crickets that came from outside the open window. He placed the book on the arm of the chair and leaned back closing his eyes for some time. He sighed, feeling content with himself. He had done well given the humble beginnings that he and his family had come from. Although he had been born in poverty; ever since his early days, Janardhan had always known that he was good-looking and that he had a sharp mind. And he had never hesitated to use both qualities to get what he wanted from life, including charming Niharika, the only daughter of the rich Zamindar of the estate on which Janardhan and his family used to live and work. To the young, ambitious Janardhan, Niharika was the perfect means to the end that he had always dreamt of for himself. He had lost no time in endearing himself to first, the Zamindar, and then to the man's daughter; never letting his contempt for the dim-witted and spoilt Niharika be seen.

Janardhan was soon married to Niharika and he came to live on the estate from the decrepit mud house where he had lived so far, on the out-skirts of the village. At first, everything seemed to be going well and Janardhan enjoyed the luxuries of his new life of abundance which was a far cry from what he had been used to. However, the novelty wore off quickly and he soon came to grudge the fact that the Zamindar continued to be in control of everyday affairs, leaving Janardhan to function merely as his secretary. The young man gritted his teeth and bade his time while continuing to humor the Zamindar and his daughter despite his misgivings. As is the norm, time went by, the Zamindar's health started to deteriorate and Janardhan lost no time in taking over control from the old man. He also ensured that Niharika's father did not get any medical treatment once the man started to ail; thus, cutting the man's life shorter than it would have been otherwise, and sooner than later, Janardhan Chowdhury was anointed the new Zamindar of the estate.

Reliving these memories, made Janardhan smile to himself. He felt no remorse – only a deep pride in all that he had achieved. He felt drowsy and was about to get up and go inside when an uncharacteristically strong breeze caused the windows above him to close with a bang thus breaking the stillness of the night and making him jump and look up at the window. The view that met his eyes caused him to draw his breath in sharply; making the sleep disappear in no time

It could not be true – he must be seeing things, he reprimanded himself. He squeezed his eyes shut, and reopened them slowly, adjusting the glasses that were perched on his longish nose, but the sight before him had not changed. *There was no mistake. There was a face at the window, and it was looking directly at him*. The woman outside had long hair, which was left loose around her oval face, the darkness made it hard to see her features although Janardhan had no doubt about her identity. The identity, coupled with the stern, unwavering gaze of the brown eyes made him squirm and made the hair on the back of his neck stand up. He opened his mouth to scream but no sound would come out. He seemed unable to move and sat paralyzed with fear while helplessly staring at the face outside the window. As he tried to scream once more, Janardhan became conscious of a constriction in his throat till the time that he could not breathe anymore, collapsing in a heap on the floor of the living room with a loud thud.

***

"Get up! Get up!!"

A woman's voice floated to his ears. Janardhan kept his eyes firmly shut. *It must be the woman that he had seen at the window. If he kept his eyes closed for long enough then perhaps, she would get tired and go away.* As these thoughts played in Janardhan's mind he felt a splash of cold water on his face which almost caused him to choke. Instinctively his eyes opened, and he sat up cursing. He looked around and saw Niharika's chubby face look at him with concern.

"Are you okay Janardhan?" asked his wife as he glared at her.

"I – I am fine…" He coughed wiping the water off his face with his palm, "What do you mean by splashing cold water on my face in the middle of the night?"

Niharika looked repentant at once. "You were unconscious, and I had heard in the village that splashing water on the face makes a person regain consciousness."

Janardhan shot his wife an incredulous glance. The woman had never displayed any presence of mind for as long as he had known her. He was about to open his mouth to give her an earful when the memory of the face in the window returned. He gave a start.

Niharika who was kneeling on the floor next him, cast him a worried look.

"What happened now?" she asked nervously placing her palm on his forehead, "Are you feeling ill?"

"Niharika…" whispered Janardhan keeping his head firmly turned away from the window above him. "Can you see if there is someone outside the window?"

Although bewildered by her husband's out-of-sorts behavior, Niharika did as she was told.

"There's no one Janardhan. Are you expecting someone?" she asked him, a tinge of concern apparent in her voice once more. "In our village everyone is asleep by 9 pm. It's past midnight now – no one should be around."

Janardhan did not reply although he cast a sideways glance towards the window. As Niharika had told him, it was empty indeed. He let out an audible sigh of relief.

"Janardhan, did you see someone outside?" probed his wife, "Is that why you lost consciousness? Do you think it was a thief? Should we call the police?" Her voice kept rising to reach a hysteric pitch with each question.

He shook his head and studied his wife's face. The beauty of her younger years had long left her and now he was looking into a chubby face with wide, unintelligent eyes that were puffy from lack of sleep.

Quickly, turning away to hide his contempt, Janardhan cleared his throat and said, "I think I saw a ghost." He stated it matter-of-factly, as one does when speaking the truth.

"A-a what?" asked his wife.

"A ghost," he repeated.

"Oh..."' she said, seeming to be at a loss for words. "W-what did it look like?" she asked after a thoughtful silence.

Janardhan paused. He wondered whether he should tell her the truth but decided against it.

"The way ghosts usually look," he said slowly getting up from the floor, supported by his wife's arm around his waist. "Large eyes like saucers, huge blood-stained teeth sharp enough to tear flesh apart from bones, floppy ears and so on..." he said making things up as he spoke. He noted the look of absolute terror on Niharika's face with some satisfaction. In the early days of their marriage, he used to find her lack of intelligence cute but now it only irritated him. He flicked her arm away from him and turned to go inside, "I am tired and am going to bed. Why don't you clean up the mess that you made here before coming inside?"

———

The soaking wet kurta stuck to his skin, his throat was parched, and he felt hot all over as the fever had returned with a vengeance. Janardhan Chowdhury made a futile attempt to sit up in bed. He looked around the spacious bedroom that was bathed with rays of the late afternoon sun, trying to locate his wife so that he could ask her for a glass of water but Niharika was nowhere to be seen. He could hear sounds of talking and laughter from the corridor outside the room and he tried to call out to her. Unfortunately, what had been intended to be a command, came out only as a feeble whisper.

Janardhan felt frustrated. In the past three months' his health had fast deteriorated, leaving him as only a shadow of his previous self. The constant flashes of fever had robbed him of his strength leaving him as a bedridden invalid, no longer able to walk without assistance. His previously obedient wife, Niharika, now treated him with thinly veiled contempt, coming around to his room only twice a day to place a tray of food before him, not bothering to see if he could feed himself or not. Janardhan knew that she was paying him back for the way in which he had treated her throughout her life. Once he was back up on his feet, then he would show her, her rightful place he would think bitterly to himself; although he knew in his heart that he would never recover again. The village doctor came around every evening to check on him and gave him a few medications which seemed to have no effect. A sense of déjà vu had settled in his mind as he recalled the last days of his dying father-in-law and the way in which he had denied the man treatment.

In three months' almost everything in his world had changed, except one – the face that he had seen for the first time at the window of the living room had continued to haunt him. He saw it in his dreams as well as while he was awake; until the time that he had reached a state of delirium where he was no longer able to distinguish between his waking and sleeping states. He saw the face everywhere and the stern, unflinching gaze that stared at him never failed to make him shiver.

He had not told anyone the truth, fearing that they would not believe him until finally one day he could take it no longer. This was while he still had had his voice about a month ago…

"Do you remember the face in the living room window that I had told you about?" he asked his wife, who stood in front of the mirror in the bedroom, combing her long hair.

"The ghost?" asked Niharika contemptuously, "Are you hallucinating again, Janardhan? The doctor said that your mind is playing tricks on you – there are no ghosts."

"Believe me Niharika," said Janardhan, desperation creeping into his voice, "Once I tell you whose face it was, then you will believe me…"

"It was the face of a ghost wasn't it?" replied his wife with a snort, "with large eyes and sharp teeth and some such nonsense. Janardhan, even the doctor is fed up with you now. I have no time to listen to your delirious blabber. I need to get back to the kitchen…"

As he watched her turn to leave the room, Janardhan blurted out what had been on his mind for days.

"Niharika, I see Nalini!"

She stopped in her tracks and turned towards him, a look of interest coming over her face. Encouraged, Janardhan continued, "I saw her face at the window that night and several times after that. She even comes into this room while we are asleep at night."

He noted with satisfaction that his wife shivered a little as she cast a doubtful glance around the room.

"I-is she in the room right now?"

Janardhan was once again beginning to enjoy himself at Niharika's expense despite his condition.

"Yes – as a matter-of-fact she is standing right behind you at this moment."

His wife leapt aside, with her hand pressed to her heart and Janardhan covered up his laugh with a cough. Niharika cast him an accusatory look.

"You will remain cruel until your dying day, won't you Janardhan Chowdhury?" she said venomously.

"We'll see how much longer you can keep this up."

Janardhan felt the blood shoot up to his brain. He wanted to go and shake the woman hard to bring her back to her senses, but he knew that he did not have the strength to get up from his bed. As he locked eyes with her, he could see that she knew it too. He let out a long sigh and lowered his eyes.

"Niharika, I am telling you the truth. Nalini is in this house. She is haunting me and after I am gone, she will haunt you and Abhishek too…"

"Why do you think that she will haunt us?" asked his wife. "We did nothing to her…besides please keep my son out of this. The poor boy has already dealt with enough because of you…"

She trailed off and the two of them exchanged knowing looks. Janardhan gulped to wet his constantly dry throat. He stared up at the ceiling and asked in a tired voice…

"What do you think Nalini wants, Niharika?"

His wife walked up to his bed and looked down on him.

"Perhaps she wants justice," she whispered, "for what you did to her…and for what you did to my father…"

Janardhan looked at her, stunned. He realized that she was more intelligent than he had credited her for. As his eyes met her fiery ones, he felt his temper return. He was used to her being subservient to him all his life but now that he was sick and weak, she dared to challenge him. He had an unbearable urge to rise and hit her hard for her insolence, however he took a deep breath and controlled his anger.

"What should I do now?" he asked his wife, searching her face for an answer and for a tinge of compassion. He found neither. Niharika pursed her lips and turned away.

"There is nothing to be done now except for repentance. You did not listen to Abhishek or me when we had tried to stop you before. So why do you ask me for an answer now?"

Janardhan watched her wide retreating back and closed his eyes.

***

"Do you recognize me? Then tell me, who am I?"

The voice was steely and disembodied; quite unlike anything Janardhan had ever heard. It sent a chilling shiver down his spine.

He stared at the face with the unwavering eyes that looked down at him. It was late at night and the household was asleep. Niharika who lay next to him was snoring peacefully in her sleep with a quilt covering her to protect her from the December cold.

"N-Nalini," he stammered returning his gaze to the hazy figure before him. Although Nalini had been haunting him for months' now, however, this was the first time that she had spoken to him. Janardhan could feel his heart beat hard. He could sense that tonight was to be different from the other nights when Nalini visited him, and this made his heart go cold with dread.

"What do you want from me? I will give you whatever you want Nalini but please leave me alone. I am very tired, I just want to sleep and to be at peace," he paused and then added for effect, "Remember, I am your father-in-law..."

The last statement had been a mistake and Janardhan realized it as soon as the words had left his mouth. A shrill laughter emanated from the figure before him causing him to sweat despite the cold, wintry night.

"Are you begging for mercy? I had begged you too, Janardhan Chowdhury – I had begged you to let me live but you did not listen to me or to Ma or to Abhishek. You were ruthless. You only wanted more money from my poor father who could not afford to give you anymore. And now you want me to think of you as my father-in-law? I will ensure that you pay for your cruelty..."

Janardhan felt streams of perspiration run down his back, he could feel his skin burning hot and his throat felt constricted. He turned towards Niharika's sleeping figure hoping that Nalini's voice would have awoken her, but the woman remained blissfully asleep. As he looked back, he discovered that Nalini's figure had disappeared, but the unbearable heat remained. It felt as though he was in an oven and someone was continuously increasing the temperature. He pushed aside the bed covers and ripped off his kurta, yet he felt no relief. Although he had been an invalid for the last month, unable to walk without assistance; Janardhan suddenly discovered that he had gained enough strength in his limbs to stand up. He immediately got out of bed and began to run. He ran as fast as he could trying to leave the blistering hot room behind him. He ran out of the house and into the dark, moonless night. He ran even though his breath had started to come in short gasps, even though his legs felt weak and even though he felt that he could not go on anymore. He continued to run for life itself, trying to get away from the burning sensation on his skin which refused to go away no matter how far he ran…

The villagers crowded around the lake that was situated at the far end of the vast Zamindar's estate. It was early in the morning and most of the crowd shivered, as much from the frigid temperature, as from the sight that was before them.

Janardhan Chowdhury's lifeless body lay head down at the edge of the pool while his body was spread out on the shore at the edge of the lake. What had led him to venture towards the lake in the middle of a cold winters' night, was inconceivable to everyone. Even more astounding were the circumstances of his death, which bore an eerie resemblance to another death in the Zamindar family not too long ago. The villagers had whispered for several months amongst themselves, about the death of Nalini Chowdhury, wife of Abhishek Chowdhury; only eight months ago.

Her body too had been discovered in a similar fashion with her head submerged in the lake, while her lifeless body lay spread out on the shore. A lot of theories had gone around the village about her death, the primary one being that the Zamindar had decided to kill her when her father could no longer pay any further dowry. However, fearing repercussions from the Zamindar; the villagers had all pretended to forget about the loss of the young life and no investigations had been made to uncover the cause of Nalini's death.

Now fate seemed to have intervened and the cruel Zamindar had met an end like that of the young, innocent girl whom he had apparently drowned in the lake in a fit of his well-known rage. Niharika stood at the edge of the lake looking down at her husband's lifeless body, covering her mouth with the pallu of her saree. She was unsure of her emotions. She did not feel any grief as she knew she should have. Instead, she felt a sense of relief. She lowered her head so that the villagers could not read her expressions. As she looked at Janardhan's body, his words rang in her ears - *Nalini is in this house. She is haunting me and after I am gone, she will haunt you and Abhishek too…*

Childhood

The train clattered into the desolate railway station at Bankura, which was deserted at 9 PM at night. The skies had opened to cause a torrential downpour to noisily splatter on the flimsy, tin roof of the station. Bhushan alighted from the train carrying his brown suitcase with him. He looked around himself uncertainly and shivered a little, which was brought on; both from the chill of the rainy night as well as with the anticipation of what awaited him. He knew that no one from house would be at the station to greet him under the given circumstances. Pulling his jacket close around his lean body, he walked towards the station master's room which was dimly lit with a single, naked light bulb.

The old station master pushed his glasses further up his nose and peered through them to look at the figure of the tall, good-looking man standing before him. The old man's face broke into a toothless smile, as he recognized Bhushan.

"Bhushan, isn't it?"

He groaned as he raised himself to a standing position. Being a small town, almost everyone knew everyone else here and the stationmaster's instant recognition of him was hardly a surprise to Bhushan.

"It's been a very long time – five years, I think, since you've last visited the village", said the old man. "You look almost the same, although you now have some grey hair and also the beard…"

Bhushan, self-consciously ran his hand through his curly hair and adjusted his glasses on the bridge of his perfectly shaped nose.

"Giridhar-kaka, how are you?"

"I am fine, my son. Although, I am very sorry about your dear father…"

Bhushan lowered his brown eyes, which threatened to well up at the reminder that he was now an orphan. He has lost his mother while he had been very young and had almost no memory of her. His father had brought up him and his younger brother – Hemant, while working as a teacher in the village school. Their family was well-loved and respected by the villagers, but Bhushan had always hated the place. It was small and limited and it suffocated him. He had yearned to get away from it in to the big, wide world which held so many opportunities for a young man like him. Soon, school was over, and Bhushan found his chance to escape the village in the form of a college admission in Kolkata. He had decided long ago that he wanted to be a doctor, and usually Bhushan always got what he wanted. He made sure that he did. He had studied hard and had gained admission to one of the reputed medical colleges in the city. Since that day, almost fifteen years ago; he had never looked back as he ascended to great heights of success in his career. Amongst these thoughts, unbidden; the vision of his ageing father and his younger brother standing next to each other – waving at him, while the train backed away from this very station; came to mind. That was the last time that he had seen his father – alive. He shook his head to chase away the memories and forced himself to speak to the elderly man before him.

"Giridhar-kaka; can you call me a rickshaw? I have no conveyance to get home."

***

It was past 11 PM and the silence of the night was only broken by the distant chirping of crickets. Bhushan was sitting on the terrace of their house which overlooked the vast paddy fields behind it. He blew out a stream of cigarette smoke as a light breeze blew through his hair. He was back after several years and as always, visiting the village brought back a deluge of memories which he preferred to keep away, as they stirred up deep-seated feelings of guilt within him. It was also one of the reasons that he hated the house. He cast a sideways glance towards his brother, Hemant who sat quietly beside him staring out into the darkness. His brother still lived in the village house along with his wife, Asha and their eight-year-old son, Bhaskar. Although Bhushan was six years older than his brother; between them, Hemant had always been the more responsible one. He had taken care of the house, the farmland as well as of their father, while Bhushan was away, busy chasing his dreams.

"Hemant…"

Bhushan paused to gather his thoughts, as Hemant turned to look at him. The large, melancholic eyes which were now fixed on his older brother had caused many women in the village to fall for Hemant during their days of youth. Bhushan observed some early tinges of grey hair at his brothers' temples. He looked away and cleared his throat

"There's something that I want to speak to you about"

"Yes?"

"Well – it's about this house"

"What about it?" asked Hemant unsuspectingly

Bhushan felt a wave of irritation run through him. At times he did not know if his brother was truly as naïve as he appeared at thirty-six, or if it was a show that he put on. He decided to get right into it without wasting anytime to set up a premise

"With Baba no more; I think we should consider selling it. You and I have discussed this before. I have already spoken with a promoter in Kolkata. According to him we should be able to make good money by selling it – in the range of 1.5-2 crores. We can split the money and you can use your share to live as you please."

A silence followed Bhushan's breathless monologue and he could feel his heart, beat fast as he waited for his brother to respond. He hoped that Hemant would not start being difficult about this. He did not have the time or patience to deal with his brother's sentimentality about the house. They had had several arguments about this in the past which had always been settled by their father weighing in, in favour of keeping the house. Now after prolonged silence from his brother, Bhushan raised his eyes to look at him. Hemant looked back silently. Bhushan's irritation grew further. He just wanted to get this over with, so that he could go back to his life in Kolkata. Staying in the village was inconvenient and he wished to get back to the comforts of his plush home. He hadn't married and lived alone, but that was the way he had intended for his life to be. He enjoyed his freedom, his successful career and the life that he had built for himself. And now, with his father no more, more than ever before was eager to cut all ties with the village. He could see no reason to prolong the inevitable decision any longer

"Well…" he said, "what do you think, Hemant? You know that I do not want to come back here again after…"

The incomplete sentence hung in the air between them as the two brothers looked at each other. If Hemant felt anything, he did not display it as his face remained an inscrutable mask

"It's been a long day today for both of us, Dada," he said finally, "why don't you go to sleep today, and we can talk about this tomorrow morning before you leave?"

Bhushan said nothing. He hated his brother's indecisive temperament. To Bhushan it spelt a weakness of character which he had always despised his brother for. Now he knew that arguing with him would be no good, so he raised himself to a standing position with a sigh and followed his brother inside the house. They stopped on the landing outside the room which Bhushan used to occupy as a child

"Asha has had your room cleaned up and your bed made. Take some rest tonight – I will see you tomorrow. Baba wanted us to keep your room exactly as it used to be while you were here…"

Hemant was about to turn away but then paused, as though considering whether to speak his next words. When he spoke, Bhushan could detect a tinge of anger in his brother's otherwise soft voice

"You know that Baba really wanted to see you. If only you had come here a few days earlier…but you were too busy as usual…", he trailed off

Bhushan instinctively opened his mouth to defend himself and then closed it again. He knew that he and his brother would never agree on many things and his resolve became stronger now

"Hemant – I think it's best that we do not talk about these things. As I said, lets sell the house, then we can go our separate ways…"

Hemant said nothing. He abruptly turned away from his brother and made his way down the stairs to the bedroom on the ground floor of the house which he occupied with Asha. Bhushan stood for a while on the landing and ran his fingers through his hair. The guilt was back – somehow this place and his brother always managed to bring it back. Selling the house was the only way forward, he told himself while entering the bedroom. He reached for the light switch which he knew was next to the door and flicked it on. As light flooded the room, he let out an involuntary gasp. Just as Hemant had mentioned, the room was the same as he remembered it from his childhood. The small, single bed at the far corner of the room, the rickety study table next to the window, the cupboard beside it followed by the bookshelf, which still held his old story books and comics. The walls were covered with the old posters of sportspersons and film stars, that he had so lovingly plastered on them, so many years ago. He walked slowly towards the study table and picked up the single photo frame that stood on it. A man gazed back at him, as he stood with his arms wrapped around two young boys on either side of him. Bhushan quickly blinked away the tears that had once again involuntarily welled up in his eyes. He slammed the photo frame, face down, and turned his back towards it. He had more practical things to worry about and could not afford to get caught in sentimentality like his brother, he told himself sternly as he lay down on the bed and closed his eyes waiting for sleep

---

He felt a light tug on his shirt sleeve. Being in a deep slumber, he flicked off the arm that tugged at him and mumbled

"Go away. Let me sleep a little more…"

But the arm persistently tugged once more at his sleeve – harder, this time

"Get up. I am hungry," said a small boys' voice next to his ear

The voice sounded familiar and taking it to be his pesky nephew, Bhaskar; Bhushan sighed irritably in his sleep. He hated kids with good reason…

"Go and ask your mother. Go away from here and stop bothering me…"

There was silence for some time and Bhushan felt relieved at successfully fending off the boy. However, his peace was short-lived as the sound of a thud followed by a crash caused him to sit upright in bed. Cursing under his breath, he switched on the light and looked around the room to identify the source of commotion as well as the culprit. A rubber ball lay innocently near his feet and the books from the bookshelf into which the ball had crashed, lay scattered around the floor.

"Bhaskar – it's no use hiding now. Come out…," he said sternly, as he saw a small figure lurking behind the bookshelf.

"I am sorry…" said the voice, "the ball slipped out of my hands"

"Come out, right now otherwise I will call your father…"

This seemed to work, and the boy sidled out of his hiding place to stand before Bhushan with a defiant expression on his small face

"Go on – call my father if you like. But he will never believe you…"

Bhushan stared dumb-struck at the nine-ish boy before him. He squeezed his eyes shut and opened them again, but the boy continued to look back at him. His throat was dry, and he gulped a few times before he was able to finally speak.

"W-what are you doing here…" he stuttered

"Well," came the response, "I live here. This is my room!"

Bhushan was silent for some more time while he contemplated the situation. He jumped, startled, as he felt a grubby hand on his shoulder. Unnoticed by him, the boy had come to sit beside him on the bed. Bhushan noticed that his feet dangled from the bed way above the floor

"Tell me – for how long will you stay here? After you go, I will get my room back…"

Left with little choice, Bhushan decided to play along and replied, "I will leave tomorrow. Your room will be yours after that", then as an after-thought, he added, "although, let me inform you that this room is mine as well."

"Oh!" said his visitor, disbelief in his voice. "If this was your room then you would come here more often, wouldn't you? I think you may be lying. Grown-ups do, you know?"

Bhushan immediately felt an urge to smack the precocious boy but clenched his fists and controlled himself. Unaware of the imminent risk that he was in, the boy continued with his chatter in a similar vein.

"Why do you have a beard? You know that it doesn't suit you, don't you?"

Bhushan's hands went self-consciously to his carefully manicured beard. The boy has no idea what he is talking about, he told himself while the boy continued…

"…and the glasses that you were wearing in the evening – why do you wear them?"

"I cannot see well without them…," replied Bhushan

"Hmmm – you must be old then. When I saw you first, you looked about fifty or sixty years old to me, but I suppose, you must be more than that?"

Bhushan continued to resist the urge to smack the kid. He prided himself on his appearance and hearing this boy tear it apart wasn't something that he took kindly to. He turned to figure beside him and opened his mouth to retaliate and then closed it again as he saw the small face, with large, brown eyes stare back at him insouciantly. He smiled involuntarily and lowered his face so as not to encourage the boy further, but it was too late

"You are smiling," said the small voice, "I know that you actually like me although you pretend not to…"

Bhushan shook his head

"No – I do not like you. In fact, I never did…"

"Why?" came the innocent response

"We – el," he paused. He did not want to hurt the kid, but he wanted to get him off his back. "For one, you talk too much…".

The boy nodded wisely.

"That's true. Baba says that as well."

At the mention of his father, Bhushan sat up.

"Where is your father? Don't you think he will be worried about you if he does not find you in bed in the middle of the night? You know that he usually checks on you, don't you?"

If the boy found it strange that Bhushan was in possession of this information then he gave no sign of it, instead he puffed out his cheeks

"No one's been talking to me since yesterday. I don't think Baba will come to look for me tonight. He's mad with me…"

"Why – what have you done?" asked Bhushan incredulously. In his view a walloping from his father, was what this kid needed badly

"You know my dog? Jojo?"

Bhushan nodded. Jojo was the 2-year-old golden retriever who lived in the house.

"Since it's been raining, so he was cold. I made a coat for him. Tell me, was I wrong?"

The large eyes looked at Bhushan, awaiting his judgement. Bhushan shook his head. "I don't see anything wrong with that," and then added, somewhat suspiciously, "…so far"

The boy's face brightened at receiving this piece of encouragement from the older man.

"You see? Grown-ups can be unreasonable, at times. Ma, Baba and everyone else is angry with me because I cut the curtains to make Jojo's coat. I thought that they could always buy more curtains but making Jojo comfortable was more important. Don't you think so?"

Bhushan covered his laughter with a cough and remained non-committal this time, not responding to the imploring look in his young visitor's eyes

The boy gave a dramatic sigh and jumped down from the bed

"All you grown-ups are the same! Anyways, I remember why I am here now – I am very hungry."

Bhushan gave him an indulgent look, with his earlier dislike for the kid rapidly fading away being replaced by a grudging fondness

"What do you like to eat?"

"I like ice-cream. I also like jalebis. Either of them would do for now"

The boy stood with his stick-like hands on his hips, as he observed Bhushan. Bhushan smiled, despite himself

"Well, I have neither with me now. So, what shall we do?"

"Then let's go out and buy some," said the boy immediately. He began to tug at Bhushan's sleeve once more

"Be reasonable," scolded Bhushan. He looked towards the clock that hung on the wall above the study-table. It showed 3 AM. "It's late at night and all shops are closed at this time. Why don't you go to bed and tomorrow morning I will buy you what you like…"

But the boy was not to be deterred. He was now pulling at Bhushan's arm trying to drag him off the bed

"I know Narayan-kaka at the local sweet shop. We can wake him up and I know that he will make jalebis for me anytime I want. He loves me very much and will not mind making jalebis even at night for me. Come on – let's go…"

Bhushan tried in vain to fend off the hand that continued to tug at him. Waking up, Bhushan opened his eyes ready to tell off the pesky boy. But no one was around him. He looked around the room which was illuminated by the early morning rays of the sun. At first, he could not remember where he was and then it all came back to him. Where he was and why. But more than that the vivid dream which had seemed so real stayed in his mind. He got up from the bed and looked behind the bookshelf to see if he could find the boy hiding there as he had in the dream. He knew that he would find nothing, but he couldn't help looking. Instead, he found a small rubber ball lying on the floor behind the shelf. Smiling to himself as he remembered the dream, he picked up a well-worn comic book from the bookshelf and started leafing through the pages when an old photograph fell out of it. He picked it up to find a boy and a golden retriever look back at him. That was him and their old family dog, Jojo. He placed the photograph in the book and decided to take it back to Kolkata with him. He took the photo frame, which still lay face down on the study table, in his hands and looked at the picture of his father, a three-year-old Hemant and the small boy that he had seen in the dream, his younger self. All of them looked back at him, with what seemed like, accusing glances, for his plan of taking their home away from them. He promptly looked away and placed the photo frame in his bag. He would keep it for the memories. A small voice in his head, the voice of the boy from his dream, spoke up, *'How many memories can you pack in a bag?'*

"Dada…", the voice from the door startled him out of his reverie. His sister-in-law, Asha, stood near the door with a cup of tea in her hands. "I've got you some tea. There is hot water in the bathroom. Why don't you take a bath and come down for breakfast before you leave?"

As Bhushan took the cup from her hands, she hesitated and then said, "Hemant is waiting for you. He said that you wanted to discuss something about the house before you leave today…"

Bhushan looked at his brother who sat across the dining table from him finishing off the last traces of his breakfast. Hemant had been avoiding eye contact with him all morning and the tension between the two of them was palpable in the room. Asha hovered around the table, trying to assuage the situation with her calm presence and tried ensuring that Bhushan was comfortable

"Dada, do you want some more tea?" she enquired, "you have a long way to go…"

Bhushan thanked her and declined the offer.

"Hemant," he said, "we need to talk before I leave…"

His brother nodded, not raising his head from the cup of tea in his hands.

"I have been thinking all of last night," he continued, "and I have reached a decision about the house…"

He saw his brother and Asha exchange looks, though neither said anything

"I think…", he paused, "that selling the house is a bad idea…"

This proclamation was followed by complete silence as the other two stared back at him for what seemed like an eternity. The only sound was the occasional crowing from outside the open window. Finally, Hemant spoke…

"Uh – so, you mean that…" he looked at Bhushan with disbelief.

"I mean that, lets keep the house as it is. And, if you and Asha agree, then I will come back home sometimes to visit all of you and the village…"

Hemant abruptly sprung up from the chair and hugged him tightly. Bhushan, although taken aback by the sudden display of affection, soon found himself hugging his younger brother back.

"Thank you so much, Dada', said Hemant through tears, "this house is what will keep memories of our childhood alive…"

Bhushan nodded, wiping away a tear from the corner of his eye.

As he let go of his brother, he felt a small hand tap him on the shoulder. Turning around, he found himself face-to-face with his nephew, Bhaskar. Now seeing the boy closely for the first time since he had arrived the previous night, he was startled by the likeness that he had to Bhushan's younger self. A pair of brown eyes stared back at him. Although Bhushan had a great dislike of children, he couldn't help feeling affection for the boy before him. He ruffled the boy's hair and said, "What is it, Bhaskar?"

"You said that you are leaving today, so got up really early and have brought something for you"

As Bhushan looked at him enquiringly, the boy produced a brown paper bag that he had been hiding behind him and presented it to Bhushan

"This is for you. Ma said that you have a long journey to make today, and I know that you will get hungry. So, I woke up Narayan-kaka in the sweet shop and asked him to make these for you. He loves me very much; you know and will do whatever I ask him to do…"

Bhushan forced himself to shake off the feeling of Deja-vu from his dream and opened the bag to find crispy jalebis inside. He looked back at the boy who was continuing with his chatter

"…I wanted to get you ice-cream as well, my other favourite food, but Ma said that it will melt soon. I have an idea though; we can go to the ice-cream shop now, and you can buy me some. I will let you eat a little as well…"

He began to tug at Bhushan's sleeve to get him out of the chair, ignoring his mothers' warnings and reminders about getting ready for school. Smiling, Bhushan got up and followed his nephew out of the house as they walked together to the ice-cream shop at the corner of the street.

The Bungalow

The Bungalow was situated in a leafy by-lane close to the centre of the city. The location was an ideal one, since one hand it provided a quiet and peace to its residents while on the other, it was a walking distance away from amenities as well as luxuries that the city of Bangalore possessed. At a first glance, the house seemed unkempt with the garden surrounding it being over-grown with weeds and the outside walls with cracks and peeling paint. However, the inside had recently been renovated, with the smell of the fresh paint on the walls still hanging around in the air around the house. The lower floor had a huge lounge which opened into a dining space with French windows which led to the backyard. To the right of the dining room was the spacious kitchen, while a broad wooden staircase was situated to its left which led to the five bedrooms upstairs. There was also an out-house situated in the garden where the elderly housekeepers; Shiv and Padma, lived. They were both locals, who claimed to have lived in the city for years. Given the size and location of the house, it was a wonder that Joy Ganguly, who was coming to the city for the first time along with his large family, was able to rent the house at an affordable price. When he had come to visit for the first time along with his wife,

Tina; the couple had been suspicious when they heard the rent.

Shiv, shuffled his feet, looked down at his torn chappals and mumbled through betel-stained, broken teeth…

"Sir, I will give you the owners' phone number. Mr. Reddy lives in America. Why don't you speak with him…?"

Tina's studied Shiv who was standing before them and for an inexplicable reason she felt a sense of unease. She couldn't place her finger on the reason, since the man was being respectful bordering on deferential; yet hearing him speak in his low, nasal voice, made a chill run down her spine. He was dressed in a blue lungi and a white banyan. His white beard stood out in stark contrast to the dark skin. She couldn't help noticing that he refused to make eye contact with them. Shiv's wife, Padma, hovered in the background with a broom in her hand pretending to clean the grounds although it was evident that her eyes were fixated on the two prospective tenants. Despite trying hard, Tina could not decipher Padma's features as the woman's face and head were covered with the pallu of the well-worn, cotton saree.

Joy had typed in Mr. Reddy's phone number in his phone which was offered to him by the housekeeper

"I see that the interior of the house has been recently renovated. When did the earlier tenants leave?" he enquired

Shiv hesitated as though weighing his words. Padma replied from behind him…

"It's been some time sir. Since Mr. Reddy and his family do not live in India, so it's hard to find new tenants quickly." She paused and added, "it will be good if you decide to come to live here though…it's been a while since a family has lived here."

Shiv tuned around at an alarming speed to give her a warning look, which caused the woman to rapidly retreat further into the shade of the banyan tree at the edge of the garden. He shouted something to her in the local language which Joy and Tina did not catch.

The Ganguly family was a large one compromising seven members; the patriarch of the household was Mr. Bhubhan Ganguly who was a retired Professor of Chemistry from a reputed college in Kolkata; his wife, Mrs. Jaya Ganguly; a homemaker, whose sharp tongue was feared by the whole household as well as by everyone who knew her. The senior Gangulys had three children: all of them boys. Their older son was Joy Ganguly, whose new job in the city of Bangalore had brought the family from Kolkata to their new abode. Joy and his wife Tina were parents to the three-year old girl, Alia. Being the eldest son of the family, Joy had always taken it upon himself to look after everyone else which had caused him to age beyond his thirty-five years. His earlier good looks were now marred by fast greying hair, thick spectacles and extra weight which was a result of spending long hours in a sedentary job. His wife, on the other hand, although the same age as Joy; was pretty and had maintained herself well. She was aware of her innocent looks and never hesitated to use it to her advantage. Joy had two younger brothers – Madhav and Sunil. Madhav had been working in a company in Bangalore for the last two years. Although he had been living in a PG so far, but with his older brother bringing the whole family to the city; he had moved into the house along with his family. Sunil was still completing college and lived in a hostel in Mumbai. However, since it was his summer holidays, so he was helping the family move in and settle down in the new city.

Bhubhan gazed out of the large window in the living room. The thick overgrowth in the garden made visibility of the road outside the house difficult. He raised his voice and called out to Shiv.

"Sir – how can I help?" came a voice from beside him almost instantly, making him jump.

"You gave me a scare," he said accusingly and then continued, "the garden is in a bad condition. You and Padma have been living here to look after the house. How can you keep it this way?"

"Sir – we will get clean it immediately," replied Shiv in his usual mild manner. "Anything else, sir?"

Bhubhan shook his head and dismissed the man. He looked thoughtfully at his retreating figure. Tina had come in with his morning tea and the newspaper. As she was setting down both on the table before him, Bhubhan addressed his daughter-in-law.

"That man, Shiv makes me feel somewhat uneasy, Tina. Do you feel the same way?"

Tina cast a quick glance around her and responded in almost a whisper.

"Baba – in fact, I was saying the same to Joy last night. He never makes eye contact, and his wife is worse; I have a feeling that she has a habit of listening at doors. We should be careful while they are in the house during the day. At night…they disappear…"

She paused and the two of them exchanged knowing looks as the words hung in the air. Tina's words were literal – although the couple served the family through the day, as soon as evening descended, they were nowhere to be found.

About a week after they had moved into the house, Jaya had taken it upon herself to enquire about their whereabouts in the evenings, to which Padma had simply replied,

"We are getting old madam. We need to rest in the evening…"

Jaya snorted irritably, "It isn't as though you are of much use during the day either. It's a pity that we are stuck with you in this house. We could find perfectly good maids if we look outside but since you live here, so none of the local people are ready to come and work for us…"

In her customary manner, Padma had not responded to this statement, and merely retreated from the master bedroom where this conversation had taken place. A further two weeks had passed now and as the family sat down for dinner one evening, the conversation had once again steered to the housekeepers

"Do you think that we should look again for a maid to come in and do some of the work for us? This is a large house, and we are a big family…", said Jaya

"But Ma, do you suppose that they will agree?" asked Tina. "After all they have been living here for a long time and we are only tenants…also, they are very efficient, if you know what I mean…"

Madhav, who was the only one of the brothers that had inherited his mother's short temper, responded…

"That couple has been getting on my nerves from the first day we moved here. The other day I was on the terrace with my friends and the woman, Padma appeared out of nowhere giving us all a scare. I find her creepier than her husband – she rarely speaks, and I am not sure if I have ever clearly seen her face…"

"Spooky…", said his younger brother Sunil. The youngest member of the family spoke the least, but his observations were usually accurate

"That's the word I had been looking for! Spooky!" replied Madhav

Bhubhan nodded slowly.

"I don't know about that, but I was amazed at Shiv's efficiency yesterday. I had asked him to clear up the over-growth in the garden in the morning and by afternoon it was done! It was a lot of work and Shiv is an old man…"

The family exchanged uneasy glances with each other. Joy, seeing the obvious discomfort on the faces of his family, quickly interjected, "we are free to get help from outside if we want to. In case they make any trouble, I will speak with Reddy…"

"Sir is there something that I can help with?" came a voice from beside Joy which made them all jump up collectively from their chairs. Shiv stood beside Joy with his head deferentially bowed. The strange thing was that no one had heard or seen him enter the room

"Goodness!" exclaimed Joy with his hand over his rapidly beating heart, "stop scaring me like that Shiv. You mustn't sneak around the house. Also, we thought that you needed to rest in the evenings and are not available, so how are you here now that it's 9 PM?"

"I am sorry I scared you sir," came the nasal response. "I was unable to sleep, so I thought of coming in to see if I could help with something. I happened to hear the discussion about getting outside help…", he paused and looked at the faces around the table, his piercing eyes pausing on each face before moving onto the next. When he continued, Shiv's voice had turned from its regular whine to one of steel which sent fingers of ice down everyone's spine. "I am afraid sir that I cannot allow that to happen in this house. Padma and I will do all the housework like we have been doing for all previous tenants for years now. So please allow us to continue conducting our duties, sir. You will not find our services to be lacking in any way…"

This monologue was followed by a stunned silence in the room as everyone waited for the other to speak. This was the most that Shiv had spoken since the Ganguly family had taken up residence in the bungalow. With the warning delivered, Shiv was again back to being his respectful self, who stood with his head bowed as though awaiting further instructions from his masters.

"Ok – ok," said Tina, trying to think about a quick way to get the man out of the room and the house. "Shiv, why don't you go and make Baba and Ma's beds and then take Baba's medicines to his room? He is done with dinner and will be going to bed now. You can leave the house after that and come back tomorrow morning."

Early the next morning, a shrill scream reverberated through the house making everyone drop their morning chores to run in the direction of the sound. Joy rushed out of the shower in the bathroom with a towel wrapped around his waist and hurried into the large master bedroom, next to the one that was shared by him and Tina, to find the rest of the household already there, sombrely gathered around the bed situated at the far end of the room. Bhubhan Ganguly lay on his back, as though in a deep, peaceful slumber while his wife stood before him; her eyes wide and her mouth hanging slightly open. Alia was clinging fearfully to her mother, Tina, while the usually resourceful Tina stood looking on helplessly as she seemed to be at a loss, for once. Sunil stood behind his mother to ensure that she did not collapse. Madhav sat on the bed next to his father, checking for his pulse. He looked up as his older brother entered the room and slowly shook his head. Joy felt dizzy as the blood drained from his head. He clutched onto his wife to avoid falling. It was a bizarre out-of-body feeling that he was experiencing at that moment, as he looked once more at the other people gathered in the room. He noticed Shiv and Padma standing near the head of the bed and even in his dazed state he found himself wondering why he hadn't seen them when he had first entered the room.

The sudden demise of the patriarch of the family had shaken the Ganguly family, with a sense of gloom replacing the earlier excitement of moving into the new city and home. The grief was compounded by a disbelief at the suddenness of the unfortunate event since Bhubhan, although elderly, had been in good health. The doctors attributed the cause of death as a heart attack while his family knew that the man had never suffered from a heart condition

"It's very unfortunate but this can happen to elderly people if they undergo a sudden shock – for example, if they see or hear something unexpected…", said the doctor to a forlorn Joy.

Still being in a state of shock himself, Joy shook his head in a resigned manner, "What kind of shock could he have had? He was asleep in his own room. In any case, it doesn't matter anymore, does it doctor?"

He thanked the doctor and led him to the front door. Just outside he spotted Padma lurking in the shadows of the banyan tree. A moment later when he looked back; she was gone, making him wonder absently whether she had been there or had he imagined seeing the old woman

---

A mere month after the demise of Bhubhan Ganguly, as the family was gradually limping back to the rhythm of regular life, misfortune befell them once more as unexpectedly as it had, the first time.

It was late evening on an uneventful Thursday and Joy was sitting on the terrace of the house smoking a cigarette. The terrace provided a good view of the city, including several of its landmark buildings which are situated near the centre of town, but Joy was not in a mental state to admire the beauty of his surroundings. The death of his father had been weighing heavily on his conscience. For weeks now, he had been fighting a battle with himself and was unable to forget that it had been his decision of bringing his family from Kolkata to Bangalore. Had he not brought them along, then his father might still have been with them today. He ran his fingers through his unruly hair and turned around to look at his mother, Jaya, who was taking clothes off the drying line behind him. Joy had noticed that his mother had been avoiding speaking with him.

"Ma…" he said tentatively not knowing what to expect. Like everyone else, Joy feared his mother's unpredictable moods. The woman grunted a response not bothering to turn and look at her son. Joy stood up and walked over to her…

"Ma, are you upset with me?" he paused and then forced himself to continue, "You haven't been speaking with me since…"

Joy stopped mid-sentence on seeing the look on his mother's face. She opened her mouth to speak and then shut it. After a moment's silence she opened her mouth again…

"If you hadn't insisted on bringing us to this house then all this would not have happened. We were living peacefully in Kolkata…"

Joy knew that his mother did not mince words, but he hadn't been prepared for the direct allegation which felt like a slap on the face. He composed himself and tried to reason…

"I only wanted for all of us to be together. This wasn't just my decision – Baba had wanted this too and I had imagined that so did you…How can you blame me entirely for it…?"

There was silence for some more time as Jaya continued removing clothes from the line. A while later she turned towards her eldest son and said firmly

 "I do not like staying in this house. I want to go back to my house in Kolkata. Can you arrange for me to return home, Joy?"

Joy was speechless for a while. He lowered his head to hide the tears that welled up in his eyes. Several emotions assaulted him at once – guilt, anger, sadness and many others which he couldn't quite place.

"Alright Ma, if you wish so then I will take you back to Kolkata next week," he said once he had gotten his voice back. His mothers' back was once again turned towards him. Knowing that the discussion was over, Joy walked rapidly towards the door of the terrace where he almost collided with Shiv, who seemed to be hiding behind the open terrace door.

"Move aside. Why do you lurk around, Shiv?" he demanded irritated, "it's damn annoying, you know?"

Joy heard a mumbled apology from Shiv as he proceeded down the stairs towards the privacy of his bedroom.

It was past 9 PM and the family was gathered at the dinner table. Tina was serving dinner, assisted by Padma, who was nowadays available in the evenings as well.

"Where's Ma?" asked Madhav looking around the room. He was used to his mother serving them dinner. "Is she ill?"

No one seemed to know where she was.

"Perhaps she is tired and is resting in her room," replied Tina. "I haven't seen her since evening and didn't want to disturb her."

"Let me go to her room and see," said Madhav. It could have been his imagination, but as he was raising himself from the chair, Madhav saw Padma freeze for a moment and then rapidly recede into the kitchen

A while later, Madhav returned to the dining room looking worried.

"Dada – I have searched the whole house, but I cannot find Ma anywhere..." he said to his older brother.

"Did you check the terrace?" asked Joy, slowly his breath catching in his throat. For no conceivable reason he felt a strong sense of foreboding.

Madhav bounded up the stairs leading to the terrace with Joy closely behind him. The rest of the family followed them with Tina carrying a scared Alia on her hip. The terrace was in darkness. Madhav flicked on the light switch which caused the single naked lightbulb to partially illuminate the large area.

"Ma…" he shouted, looking around him

"Ma – are you here?" shouted Joy as he fought to keep his voice even, so that he did not alarm his family any further. His eyes went involuntarily to the clothing line, and he observed a few clothes still hanging on it. The bucket with the dry clothes lay beneath the line, exactly where it had been during his brief discussion with Jaya earlier that evening. He knew that it was unlike his mother to leave a job that she had started, unfinished. "Ma…" he screamed, his voice ringing with panic, this time.

"Dada…" screamed Sunil from the far corner of the terrace. "Come quickly…"

The family assembled around Sunil who was bending over Jaya, who lay huddled on the ground. She seemed to have collapsed and as Sunil raised her head and put it in his lap, he observed that her eyes were closed. She looked peaceful and serene, just as Bhubhan Ganguly had in his death.

Tina was in the local grocery shop to buy vegetables when she was approached by a middle-aged lady who lived in their neighbourhood and whom she so far knew by face only.

"You live in the bungalow beside the banyan tree, don't you?" asked the lady by way of initiating a conversation with Tina. "I am Savitri. We live two houses ahead of you in the same lane. My family has lived here for years now."

With the stress of moving into the new city, followed by the consequent misfortunes that had befallen the family, the normally sociable Tina hadn't had an opportunity to make any friends. She welcomed this opportunity to make an acquaintance and introduced herself. Savitri seemed to be watching her through her gold-rimmed old-fashioned glasses, in a way that made Tina uncomfortable. Seeming to make an instant decision, the woman reached for Tina's hand and whispered urgently in her ear…

"If you have finished your shopping then come to my house for some tea. I need to tell you something…"

Taken aback by this sudden show of familiarity from the stranger, Tina hesitated, but Savitri tugged at her arm

"It's important for you to know something – come on!"

A while later Tina was seated on an uncomfortable wooden sofa with a cup of warm tea in her hands. She noticed with some disapproval that the living room of Savitri's large house was unkempt and cluttered. Savitri's voice drew Tina's attention from her surroundings to the sharp eyes that were set in the shrewd face of the woman seated before her. Having missed hearing some of what Savitri had been saying so far Tina politely brought her attention back

"…I have wondered if you have conducted a background check about your house before you moved into it. I am sure that you must know that the house has been vacant for quite a long time now…"

"Oh," replied Tina with some surprise. "We had spoken over the phone with the owners who now live in the US. Also, Shiv had told us that the previous owners had vacated the house only a few months back."

Savitri responded to this in a flat voice. "Tina, they are lying to you. No one has lived in that house for over five years now."

"B-but" stammered Tina. "Shiv and Padma live in the outhouse and work for us. I don't think that they would lie to us…"

An unmistakable look of horror crossed her hostess's face

"Trust me; no one lives there. The house has been vacant for years…"

Tina jumped up from the sofa.

"That's enough." she said holding out her palm towards Savitri to stop her from speaking further. "I do not know you and I am not sure what your intentions are, but I will believe what I see…"

She turned around to leave the house when Savitri's words caused her to freeze in her steps.

"I felt that it was my responsibility as a neighbour to let you know the truth, Tina. You and your family are not safe in that house. Believe me when I say that NO ONE has lived in that house for at least five years now. The house is supposed to be haunted. Several years ago, a family lived there and during a thunderstorm a large tree had fallen on the house, killing all it's five members, including the aged couple who looked after the house. We had witnessed that event…"

Tina slowly turned to face Savitri whose words made the hair stand up on the back of her neck

"And..?" she whispered, not knowing what to expect

"And – since then two other families had come to live in the house before you. In each case, the oldest member of the family died for no apparent reason and the trend continued till they realized what was happening and finally left…"

Tina's eyes grew large with fear as she stared at Savitri who lowered her voice

"I know that you too have had sudden deaths in your family after moving into the house. Those were not natural deaths although they might have seemed so…"

She paused and then looked straight in Tina's eyes

"Get your family out of that house as fast as you can, Tina. If you don't, then the deaths will not stop until everyone of you is finished."

Tina clutched at her throat with fear.

"Joy is now the oldest in the house. D – Does that mean that – that now his life is in danger?"

Savitri nodded slowly with sympathy showing on her wrinkled face.

"Tina – know this, Shiv and Padma are not who you think they are. They do not exist. Just listen to me and leave the house as soon as you can. Then you will all be okay…"

Tina stood rooted to the spot for a while and then turned and ran out of Savitri's house. She reached the gate of their bungalow, gasping for breath when Alia came running out of the house with tears streaming down her face.

"Mamma – Mamma – come fast. Baba isn't waking up…"

Tina stared at her daughter's face and then out of the corner of her eye she saw Padma. For the first time she caught a glimpse of the woman's face beneath the pallu. She smiled at her baring sharp, white teeth. A sudden darkness engulfed her as Tina collapsed on the ground, unconscious. The last thing in her mind before losing consciousness was that she would have to get her family out of the house as Savitri had mentioned.

About the Author

Sumana Roy Chowdhury

Sumana is a Technology leader, currently leading a research group in an organization in Bangalore. She has been educated in India and USA and possesses an undergraduate degree from IIT Kharagpur and a PhD degree from the University of Akron, USA. She is an author of 10 scientific journals, over 20 international patents and one scientific textbook chapter. She enjoys writing short stories and has had some of her works published on writing portals, such as spark magazine, muse india and quest penmanship. Besides, she has published a book 'Together at last' in 2021 with Srishti Publishers.